This Walker book belongs to:

_____

_____

_____

For Charlie

First published 1998 by Walker Books Ltd, 87 Vauxhall Walk, London SE11 5HJ

This edition published 2010

2 4 6 8 10 9 7 5 3 1

© 1998 Penny Dale

The right of Penny Dale to be identified as author/illustrator of this work
has been asserted by her in accordance with the Copyright, Designs and Patents Act 1988

This book has been typeset in Stempel Schneidler

Printed in China

British Library Cataloguing in Publication Data:
a catalogue record for this book is available from the British Library

ISBN 978-1-4063-2885-1

www.walker.co.uk

Ten Play Hide-and-Seek

Penny Dale

WALKER BOOKS
AND SUBSIDIARIES
LONDON · BOSTON · SYDNEY · AUCKLAND

T here were ten in the bed and the little one said,

"Let's play hide-and-seek!"

So the little one counted and the others went to hide.

"One, two, **three, four, five** ...

six, seven ... eight, nine and ...

ten!

Ready or not...

Here I come!" the little one said.

He looked under the bed and inside the drawer.

He went to the cupboard and opened the door.

BOO!

"Found you, Ted!" the little one said.

"That makes two of us!" the little one said.

"Now let's find the others."

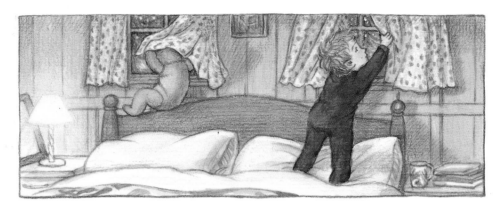

They looked behind the curtains,

under the pillows,

inside the box of bricks.

They looked and they listened, and ...

BOO! "Found you, Sheep!"

BOO! "Found you, Rabbit!"

BOO! "Found you, Zebra!"

"That makes five of us," the little one said.

"Now let's find the others."

They looked behind the coats,
under the table,

among the pots and the pans.
They looked and they looked, and …

BOO! "Found you, Hedgehog!"

BOO! "Found you, Bear!"

BOO! "Found you, Croc!"

BOO! "Found you, Nellie!"

"That makes nine," the little one said.
"Let me see. Someone's still missing...
Who can it be?"

"Not me,"
said Croc.

"Not me,"
said Nellie.

"Not me,"
said Hedgehog.

"Not me," said Bear.

"Not me," said Rabbit.

"Not me," said Zebra.

"Not me," said Sheep.

"Not me," said Ted.

Then a teeny little voice squeaked ...

"It's meeeeeee!"

"Found you, Mouse!" the little one said.

"Now we can **all** go to bed."

"Night-night, Ted. Night-night, Zebra.

Night-night, Rabbit, Bear and Sheep.

Night-night, Hedgehog. Night-night, Croc.

Night-night, Nellie, Mouse and me!"

"Night-night, everyone,"
the little one said.

Night-night, sleep tight,
ten in the bed.